I'm Not Sharing with You!

PRIVATE
STEPSISTERS ONLY!

BY LILY GOOD

Written by Julie Sykes
Illustrated by Jess Mikhail

Published by Pearson Education Limited, Edinburgh Gate, Harlow, Essex, CM20 2JE.

www.pearsonschools.co.uk

Text © Julie Sykes 2013

Original illustrations © Pearson Education Limited 2013
Illustrated by Jess Mikhail, United Agents

The right of Julie Sykes to be identified as author of this work has been asserted by her in accordance with the Copyright, Designs and Patents Act 1988.

First published 2013

17 16 15 14 13
10 9 8 7 6 5 4 3 2 1

British Library Cataloguing in Publication Data
A catalogue record for this book is available from the British Library

ISBN 978 0 435 14367 1

Printed and bound in the UK by Ashford Colour Press.

Acknowledgements
We would like to thank Bangor Central Integrated Primary School, Northern Ireland; Bishop Henderson Church of England Primary School, Somerset; Bletchingdon Parochial Church of England Primary School, Oxfordshire; Brookside Community Primary School, Somerset; Bude Park Primary School, Hull; Carisbrooke Church of England Primary School, Isle of Wight; Cheddington Combined School, Buckinghamshire; Dair House Independent School, Buckinghamshire; Glebe Infant School, Gloucestershire; Henley Green Primary School, Coventry; Lovelace Primary School, Surrey; Our Lady of Peace Junior School, Slough; Tackley Church of England Primary School, Oxfordshire; and Twyford Church of England School, Buckinghamshire for their invaluable help in the development and trialling of the Bug Club resources.

CONTENTS

CHAPTER 1
TREASURE

My family is growing. At first it was me, Mum and my little brother Dan. Then I got a dad. His name's Alex, and he's a music teacher. He came to live with us when he married my mum. Alex has a drum kit which is so big that it fills the whole of our spare room.

Next, I got a new sister. Tara. She's Alex's daughter. She's eleven, which is one year older than me, but you wouldn't believe it. The way she acts you'd think she was ten years older.

When she first came to visit, I asked if she wanted to play in our garden and Tara looked at me like I was some grubby little kid!

"I never play in gardens. What if I got injured?" she said. "It would ruin my dancing career."

I suppose she's got a point. Gardens are dangerous places. What if she'd had so much fun in ours that she'd cracked her face smiling?

MUM, DAN AND ME

ALEX AND TARA

+

= ?

My mum thought I'd be thrilled to have a stepsister.

"Isn't it exciting!" she gushed. "Now Alex is living with us, Tara is going to come and stay at the weekends."

"Noooo!" I wailed loudly. "I would rather eat cold lumpy custard for the rest of my life than put up with Tara for a whole weekend."

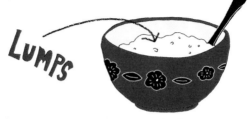

LUMPS

Mum shot me a look. I could tell she wasn't pleased.

"Anyway," I rushed on, "she can't. We don't have a spare room any more. It's got Alex's drum kit in it."

"Tara can share your room," said Mum. "It'll be a great way for you girls to get to know each other properly."

"I know plenty about Tara and I know I don't like her," I squeaked. "She's not sharing my room."

Mum folded her arms across her chest and glared at me.

"Lily Good, that is not nice."

It's so unfair. Tara isn't nice either. She's always boasting about how brilliant she is and how many dance competitions she's won. Then I had a thought.

"What about Tara's dance class?" I asked. "That's on a Saturday. She'll have to miss it if she stays here."

"Tara's class has been moved to Thursdays," Mum countered.

Arguing clearly wasn't getting me anywhere so I tried my sad face. I turned my mouth down and hung my head pretending I was really upset.

"I'd love to share with Tara." The words caught in my throat and I even managed to squeeze a tear from my eye. "Only, there isn't room. You'll have to find somewhere else to put her."

I wasn't fooling Mum.

"Tara is sharing your room and you will be nice to her or I'll ground you for life."

She was bluffing about the life bit. I bet she wouldn't want me still hanging around when I was thirty – but she could easily ground me for a week.

"If you ground me, I'll miss Harry's birthday party at the Sky Riders Theme Park," I protested.

"Well, you'd better be nice then," said Mum sweetly.

WOBBLY LIP

The weekend came round far too quickly. On Thursday evening Mum started preparing for Tara's visit.

"Lily, come and help me move your bed to make room for the camp bed," she shouted down the stairs.

My bed is brilliant. It has four knobs that are great for hanging things on. I've strung a net across the end ones and filled it with all my soft toys. I've got sixty-three but Mr Flopsy is my all-time favourite. He's a teddy bear with soft brown fur and a lopsided smile. He's ten like me and a little threadbare. Not that I'm threadbare but I can guess how he feels.

MR FLOPSY

63 CUDDLY FRIENDS

"It's a good thing your bed is on wheels or it would be too heavy for us to move," said Mum as we heaved my bed out of the way. She was red in the face and puffing like a factory chimney.

PUFF
PUFF

I was about to reply that if we couldn't move it, then Tara would have to sleep somewhere else, when I remembered Harry's birthday party and I snapped my mouth shut like a crocodile.

SNAP!

We pushed my bed to the other side of my room and uncovered a rectangular shape of darker carpet and a pile of things on the floor.

"Treasure!" Mum exclaimed.

FLIP FLOP

NOTEBOOK

CASH

NOTEBOOK

There was a blue and white flip flop which I had been trying to find for ages, a coin covered in fluff and a pretty notebook with a lily on the cover that I'd forgotten about.

"Is that your diary?" Mum asked. "Better put it somewhere safe." And she went off to get the camp bed.

I stared around. My room looked wrong
with the bed against the opposite wall and
I had a sudden urge to shove it against
the door so that no one could get in.
Then Tara would have to share with Dan.
Brilliant idea! I was just about to move it
when I remembered what Mum had said,
and I pictured my friends at Harry's party
WITHOUT me.

That's when I had another brilliant idea.

I would write a guide in the notebook
to help me be nice to Tara. I hunted in my
desk for my favourite pink gel pen.

HARRY

Opening my book I wrote on the
first page:

HOW TO BE
A GOOD
STEPSISTER

A GUIDE
BY LILY GOOD

Did you see what I did there? How to
be a *Good* Stepsister.

PRIVATE

STEPSISTERS ONLY!

DO NOT COMPLAIN WHEN YOU HAVE TO SHARE YOUR ROOM. IT MIGHT LEAD TO HIDDEN TREASURE.

MY FIRST TIP

Maybe I'll share my guide with Tara. She could add some tips of her own – if only she'd stop thinking about dancing long enough to write them down.

CHAPTER 2
TARA ARRIVES

After school on Friday, Alex went to collect Tara, and while he was gone Mum told me to empty a drawer in my room so she'd have somewhere to put her things.

"But what about my things?" I asked.

"Move them to your wardrobe," said Mum. "There's plenty of room inside."

Mum obviously hasn't opened my wardrobe lately. It's so jam-packed full, there's not enough room for one tiny ant.

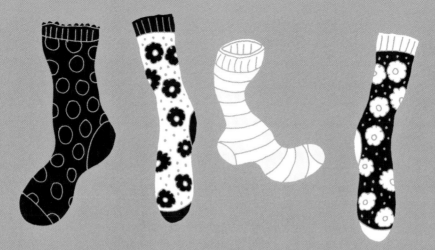

My chest of drawers wasn't much better. I opened all five of the drawers but they were bursting with clothes. I started to empty the sock drawer, making a pile of socks on my desk, but soon my desk was covered in socks and I didn't have anywhere to write. That wouldn't do.

Quickly, I shoved the socks back in the drawer. I still hadn't made space for Tara when Mum called up the stairs that she was here, which set me in a panic until I remembered she was only staying for two nights. She didn't really need a drawer. She could live out of her bag. With legs like a wobbling jelly, I went downstairs to meet her.

Mum, Dan and I lined up on the drive while Alex parked the car. It must have looked like we were waiting to meet royalty. Tara clearly thought so. She climbed out of the car, nodded at Mum and swept indoors leaving Alex to bring in her three bags. Yes, *three* bags, one of them with wheels on the bottom.

"Is Tara moving in?" I asked.

"Why doesn't she help Alex?" Dan added quickly.

"Be nice," hissed Mum. "Tara's still getting used to her dad living with us."

I hung back to help Alex. I was worried he was going to explode. He was bright red and panting heavily.

In the hallway, Tara stood as stiff as a broom handle while Mum hugged her. I kept thinking that if Alex did explode, we could turn Tara upside down and use her long wavey brown hair to sweep up the mess.

"Welcome home, Bunny," puffed Alex, dumping Tara's bags on the floor.

PRINCESS
TARA

Bunny? Seriously? I nearly choked with laughter.

Tara's face darkened until she was more grizzly bear than fluffy wuffy bunny.

"Where's my room?" she asked, pulling away from Mum.

"You're sharing with Lily," said Mum. "Lily, show Tara where she's sleeping."

Tara breathed in sharply. "Sorry, but I must have misheard. I thought you said I was sharing with Lily."

Mum shuffled nervously. "I did."

"I don't think so," said Tara. "I need my own space. Besides, Lily's much younger than me."

"A year," said Alex, ignoring Tara's ice-cold glares that had frozen everyone else.

"Tara can have my room. I'll share with Lily," Dan piped up.

"Thanks Dan, but it'll be fun for the girls to share," said Alex. "It'll give them a chance to get to know each other."

Tara and I exchanged a look. Clearly we were as enthusiastic about getting to know each other as a mouse making friends with a python.

In silence she followed me up the stairs.

"In here," I said, pushing open the door to my room. "That's your bed there."

"I wouldn't have come if I'd have known I was camping," said Tara, glaring at the camp bed. She turned around slowly, her lips curling with scorn as she took in my room.

"How old are you?" she asked, staring at my net of cuddly toys.

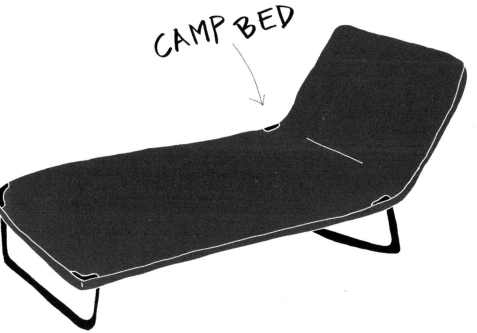

CAMP BED

Just then Alex and Dan came in with Tara's luggage.

Tara flashed Dan a huge friendly smile. "Thanks Dan. You're a star."

Dan went pink with pleasure.

"Dinner's in an hour. It'll give you two some time to get to know each other," said Alex.

Putting down the bags, he made a speedy exit.

Dan hovered, staring adoringly at Tara with huge puppy eyes.

I cast around for my bin because if he kept that up, I was going to be sick.

Suddenly Tara fixed Dan with a steely look. Lowering her voice she said, "What are you staring at, squirt? Hop it."

She might as well have kicked him. I opened my mouth to protest but Dan had already scarpered and now Tara was turning on me.

"Where do I put my things?" she asked.

Good question. Tara needed a whole room just for her luggage.

"Erm, Mum said to give you one of my drawers," I muttered. "I was just about to empty one when you arrived."

"Forget it," said Tara, striding over to my chest of drawers. "I'll do it myself."

PUPPY EYES

Sliding open the top drawer, she scooped up all my socks and carried them to the desk. Leaning over, she opened the window and flung them outside. I couldn't move. My feet seemed glued to the floor.

"These can go too. Baby stuff," said Tara, marching towards my cuddly toys.

"Stop!" I said but it was too late. Mr Flopsy, five teddies, a black and white cat and Tiny Mouse were already free-falling from the window.

"You're mean!" I yelled. "You're the nastiest, most spiteful …"

I caught sight of my guide and stopped. Visions of the Sky Riders Theme Park floated past my eyes. What would I gain from telling Tara she was horrible? From her smug smile, she knew it already.

Snatching up my guide and pen, I stomped downstairs to the garden. Mr Flopsy was face down on the grass. I inspected him for damage but luckily there wasn't any. Tiny Mouse was stuck in a bush with two pairs of stripy socks.

I gathered up my things which were strewn around the garden, then sat down, opened up my notebook and began to write:

REMEMBER TO EMPTY A DRAWER FOR YOUR STEPSISTER BEFORE SHE ARRIVES.
IT WILL SAVE HER DOING IT FOR YOU.

CHAPTER 3
PINEAPPLE CHUNKS

Mum and Alex had organised a "family night in": dinner first, then sharing a big tin of chocolates while we watched a DVD.

"Lovely," said Tara, smiling at Mum and Alex when they told us about it.

"Can we watch Karate Kangaroo?" asked Dan.

I groaned. Don't get me wrong. I loved Karate Kangaroo the first time I saw it. I loved it the second time too. I also quite enjoyed it for the third time. But we've seen it five times now and there's only so much of a karate kicking kangaroo that a girl can take.

"Tara can choose the film this time," said Mum quickly.

A funny smile played on Tara's lips.

"I'd really like to watch Karate Kangaroo," she said.

Dan was ecstatic.

"You'll love it," he told her. "It's the funniest film ever."

Mum looked pretty pleased too. For an awkward moment I thought she was going to hug Tara but then she and Alex went to the kitchen to finish preparing the meal. As soon as the door closed behind them, Tara narrowed her eyes.

"Spare me!" she said scornfully. "So what do you do for fun around here?"

Dan looked confused so I sent him off to get the DVD. I swear he sleeps with it under his pillow. Tara put the television on and cranked up the volume. I guess it was her way of telling me not to bother talking to her.

It was pizza for tea. I could smell it cooking. My favourite is four cheese. It has four different types of cheese, obviously, and best of all is the gooey mozzarella. I could also smell garlic bread. By the time Mum called us all to the dining room, I was drooling as badly as our granny's ancient dog.

"Yummy," I said, pulling out a chair.

The table was heaving with bowls of salad, cherry tomatoes, garlic bread and two huge red pepper and pineapple pizzas. Wait! That wasn't right.

"Shall I go and get the four cheese?" I asked Mum.

Mum handed the pizza wheel to Alex for him to start cutting.

"There isn't anything else," she said.

"But we always have four cheese."

WRONG!
WHERE IS MY FOUR CHEESE?

Mum sent me a sharp look.

"Tonight we're having a change. Red pepper and pineapple is Tara's favourite."

"Aw! Thanks!" said Tara, sweetly.

"You're welcome," said Mum.

Tara took two slices of pizza and piled her plate with garlic bread. "Mmm, this is delicious."

"What am I supposed to eat?" I asked. "You know I don't like pineapple."

"Don't be a baby, Lily," said mum. "You can pick the pineapple off."

"But it makes the pizza taste funny."

Tara swallowed down a lump of pizza and licked her lips.

"Lily, you're funny," she giggled, and I could tell from her eyes she didn't mean it in a good way.

"Yeah, really funny," I agreed, taking the slice of pizza Alex was holding out to me. I picked at the horrible chunks of pineapple, piling them into a lumpy mound on my plate.

EVIL PINEAPPLE

The sight of them alone was enough
to put me off eating. Tara was chomping
away like a horse. She kept shooting me
that smug smile of hers. A red mist of rage
swirled past my eyes. Tara thought I was
funny, did she? Well, let's see how funny
she found me when I dropped lukewarm
chunks of pineapple down her neck.
Scooping them up in my hand, I stood
up. Mum was watching me with a slightly
puzzled look on her face.

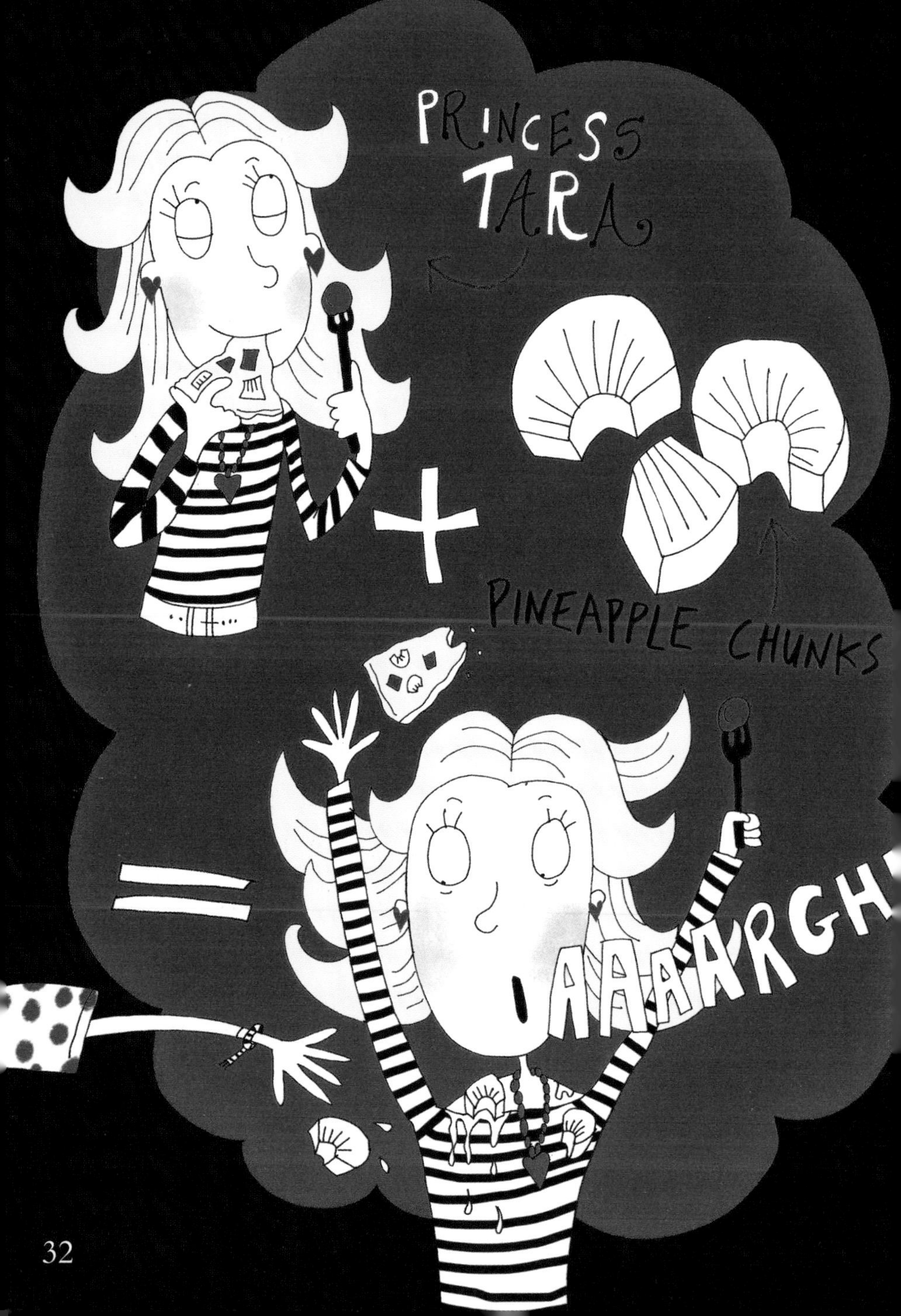
PRINCESS TARA
+
PINEAPPLE CHUNKS
=
AAAARGH

"Lily," she said, with a note of anxiety.

It was so tempting. I'd be the one with the smug smile when Tara had pineapple chunks sliding down her top. I stopped.

I'd also be the grounded one who was missing at Harry's party. Keeping my hand tightly closed, I went to the kitchen and dumped the pineapple in the bin. The only good thing about Tara's visit was that Mum let us off helping with the washing-up.

"We take it in turns to clear the table and stack the dishwasher," Mum explained to Tara. "But seeing as this is your first weekend here, your dad and I will do it tonight. Lily, go and set up the DVD."

"Dan likes to do that," I said. He's been working the DVD player since he was big enough to hold the remote control without sucking it.

"That's all right, Lily. You can do it this time. I said I'd show Tara my goldfish," said Dan quickly.

CHIPS

Dan and Tara disappeared upstairs. I went to the lounge and set up.

A short while later, Tara came back. She threw herself down in Mum's favourite armchair and began reading a celebrity magazine. A long while later, Mum and Alex came in carrying cups of coffee. Mum looked at Tara, opened her mouth, then closed it and went to sit next to Alex on the big settee.

"Where's Dan?" asked Mum.

"In his room," said Tara, without even looking up.

Suddenly I felt uneasy. It wasn't like Dan to go missing when we were about to watch a film.

"I'll get him," I said, jumping up. I ran upstairs and burst into his room. Dan was sitting at his desk with his nose glued to his fish bowl. He was mumbling something softly.

"Are you all right?" I asked.

"Yes," he said, his eyes fixed to the glass bowl. "But Chips isn't. It's lucky that Tara knows so much about fish. I might not have found out until it was too late."

"Found out what?" I said, not following.

"Chips isn't well." Dan swallowed a sob. "Tara is fish monitor at her school so she knows all about them. She said I haven't been talking to Chips enough. Fish have feelings. They get lonely and sick if you don't give them enough attention. Tara said I must talk to Chips for at least half an hour every day or else he could die."

"Tara said that?" My hands clenched into white fists.

Dan kept his face squashed against the goldfish bowl.

"Tell Mum to start the film without me. I'm going to spend the evening here."

Taking a deep breath, I squatted next to Dan. For a few minutes I peered into the fish bowl with him.

"You know what?" I said at last. "Chips can't be that lonely. You always talk to him when you feed him, don't you?"

Dan nodded earnestly.

"Well, I think he's tired, not ill. Why don't you come and watch the film and let Chips get some rest."

"Really?" asked Dan.

"Definitely," I said.

To calm down I watched Chips swim ten laps of his bowl before I followed Dan downstairs. It was that or go and write in my notebook. And somehow I didn't think that … "Shove pineapple chunks down your stepsister's top whenever you get the chance" … was quite in the spirit of how to be a good stepsister.

CHAPTER 4
EARTHQUAKE

LILY LIKES →

WARM ANI
COSY

Bedtime caused yet more issues. Tara showered first and used up all of the hot water.

"It's because she's an only child," Mum explained. "She'll soon get the hang of sharing."

Even though I doubted that, I kept my mouth firmly shut. Somehow I also managed not to say anything when Tara poked fun at my patterned pyjamas.

"Teddies, at your age, Lily! Do all your little friends wear stuff like that?"

TARA LIKES

FRILLY AND CHILLY

"At least we don't freeze in the winter," I said, eyeing her frilly, short-sleeved pyjamas.

I climbed over Tara's bags and into bed. Normally I'd take Mr Flopsy with me but tonight I'd hidden him under my bed.

Tara kicked the door shut, plunging the room into darkness.

"I always leave that open," I said, sitting up quickly.

"Well, I want it shut." Tara fumbled around catching her breath sharply when she stubbed her toe on the end of the bed.

Luckily it was too dark for her to see me grinning. The bed creaked as she lay down. It creaked some more as she rolled over. Then she turned back again. There were lots of squeaks and groans until finally she sat up and switched on the lamp on my table.

"It's no good. I can't sleep here. It'll ruin my back and I have a very important dancing competition next week."

"We've got an inflatable bed, but the camp bed's more comfortable," I said.

"I'm not sleeping on an inflatable," said Tara crossly. "I'll just have to sleep in your bed."

She shuddered slightly as if the thought repulsed her.

TARA LIKES

"Forget it," I said, rolling over to face the wall.

"I mean it, Lily. I can't sleep here. It's making my back ache," Tara whined.

"Harry always has the camp bed when he sleeps over and he never complains."

"Is Harry a dancer?" Tara demanded.

"Er, no, but he's very good at football."

"Football! So, that matters because ...?" Tara's voice was heavy with sarcasm.

Silly me! I suppose comparing dance to football was like comparing a racehorse to a hairy pony. Or comparing a totally spoilt brat like Tara to any one of my caring and generous friends, but of course I couldn't say that. Instead I snatched up my pillow and got out of bed.

HARRY LIKES

"All right! We'll swap beds, but you're not having my pillow."

"Like I'd want your pillow," said Tara, grabbing the two new ones Mum had given her.

As she leaned over to switch off the light, she saw my notebook on the desk. Her face softened.

"That's pretty," she said. "I like the flower. It's a lily, isn't it?"

I nodded, feeling slightly suspicious at her sudden change of tone.

"Is it your diary? I keep one too." Tara dived into one of her bags cluttering up my floor. She looked almost friendly as she held up a blue book with a daisy pattern. "I forgot to write in it. Seeing yours has just reminded me."

Sitting cross-legged on the bed, Tara started writing in her own diary. My heart thundered in my chest. I wanted to tell her about my guide on how to be a good stepsister. Then maybe she'd realise it wasn't easy for me either. I was just drawing breath to speak when she snapped her diary shut, shoved it back in her bag and switched off the light.

"I haven't finished!" I exclaimed

Actually I hadn't even started. So much had happened this evening, I wasn't sure where to begin.

"Too bad," said Tara, climbing into my bed. "I'm tired. Dancers need their sleep."

Thoughts were buzzing in my head like angry wasps. I had to write them down or I'd end up shouting at Tara. Quietly I rummaged in the drawer of my desk for a torch and carried it back to the camp bed. It wasn't easy writing under the duvet by torch light. As my hand moved across the page, there was suddenly a loud creak and the bed shook.

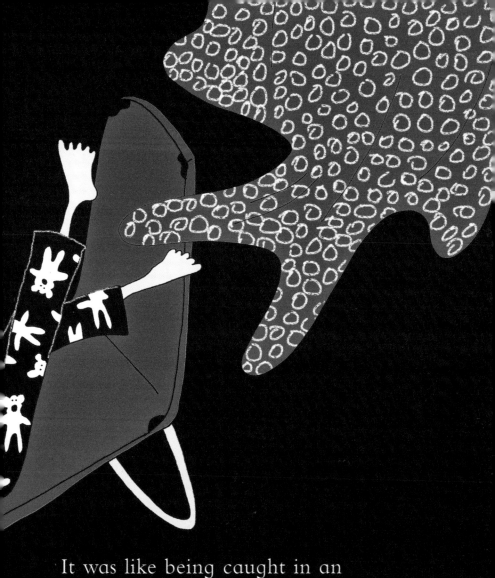

It was like being caught in an earthquake. The bed shuddered some more and then suddenly folded, almost gobbling me up. I only just managed to throw myself clear. As the bed snapped shut, I rolled into the door.

"Ouch!" I said, rubbing my head.

Footsteps pounded along the corridor. Mum threw open the door, almost squashing me flat.

"Lily Good," she shouted. "Get back to bed. If there's any more of this nonsense, then I'm grounding you for a month."

I snapped my mouth shut like a crocodile!

CHAPTER 5
AN EARLY MORNING WASH

It felt weird sleeping on the camp bed, as though I was the visitor. It made me wonder how I'd feel if I was Tara. It's not easy, living away from your dad.

The next morning I was woken by someone creeping into the room. It had to be Dan. He was as quiet as an elephant in boots as he picked his way across the floor. There was a dull thud. Dan gasped, there was another thud and then Tara started screaming. I leapt up and switched on the light. Tara was trapped in the bed by Dan who was clutching a half-empty fish bowl. There was water everywhere. Poor Chips must have felt seasick the way his bowl was moving, especially when Tara shoved Dan off her.

50

She sat up, her long hair sticking to her face as she clutched the sodden duvet.

"Get out!" she screamed.

Dan's eyes were wide with fright. "Stop shoving me or I'll spill Chips on you."

"Aaaargh! Get the fish out of here now," shrieked Tara.

Honestly. From the fuss she was making you'd have thought she was talking about a girl-chomping piranha, not a teensy goldfish too small to gobble a fly.

I prised the goldfish bowl from Dan's tight grip and put it on my desk.

He moaned. "Sorry, Tara. I thought you were Lily."

Tara's eyes narrowed. "That's how you normally wake her, by pouring fishy water over her head?"

"I was only showing her Chips. Do you think he's looking sick this morning?"

If anyone looked sick, it was Tara. Her little game had totally backfired. I had to swallow hard to stop the laughter threatening to explode from me.

"Chips looks fine," I said, "but I think he'd be happier back in your room."

Alex and Mum came in see what all the noise was about. Tara turned bright red when Dan explained everything.

Alex took her away for a little chat, while Mum gathered up the wet bedding and went downstairs.

I got dressed and went to the kitchen for breakfast.

Mum was frying some eggs on the hob. When Tara and Alex finally came downstairs, they sat opposite each other at the table. Tara's hair was a mass of brown waves.

"It's not fair," she whined. "Lily's bedroom isn't big enough for two beds. Besides, we need our own space."

Alex let out a patient sigh.

"It's good for you girls to share and get to know each other."

I sat down between them.

"Sharing's a bad idea," I said to Alex. "How would you feel about sharing your bedroom with someone you hardly knew?"

"Lily has a point," said Mum. She served up the eggs with a pile of freshly-made toast and called for Dan to join us. "Tara's a part of this family. She should really have her own room."

"Well, we don't have a spare one," said Alex, firmly.

Thoughtfully I speared my egg with a fork. Golden yolk spilled onto the plate.

"Actually, we do," I said hesitantly. "It's just full of your stuff."

There was a long silence then Alex looked at Mum.

"I could move my drums into the garage. But you'd have to leave your car on the drive."

Tara sat very still and my heart beat faster for her.

"No problem," said Mum. "Tara's far more important than a silly old car. Eat up, everyone. We'll shift things around straight after breakfast."

"Hooray!" I cheered.

Tara's eyes met mine. She stared at me for a moment and then she grinned. I smiled back at her. We were allies.

The truce lasted until Mum asked for volunteers to do the washing up. Tara stood up very quickly.

"Not me," she said. "I need to pack my things ready to move into my new room."

Well, she did bring three bags with her.

Dan said he needed to check on Chips, and Alex claimed he was too busy, now he had drums to dismantle. That left me, but I didn't mind. By the time I'd finished clearing up, Tara had moved out and my room was back to normal.

My guide lay on the desk. I wondered if I'd need it now. But there's more to being a stepsister than sharing a room. Tara and I still had lots to learn. So I picked up my pink gel pen and added my newest tip:

IT'S BETTER TO FIGHT ALONGSIDE YOUR STEPSISTER THAN AGAINST HER.

Then I went to help her unpack in her new room.